Adam's War

Adam's War

SONIA LEVITIN

PICTURES BY *Vincent Nasta*

Dial Books for Young Readers « New York

Published by Dial Books for Young Readers
A Division of Penguin Books USA Inc.
375 Hudson Street
New York, New York 10014
Text copyright © 1994 by Sonia Levitin
Pictures copyright © 1994 by Vincent Nasta
All rights reserved
Designed by Heather Wood
Printed in the U.S.A.
First Edition
1 3 5 7 9 10 8 6 4 2

Library of Congress Cataloging in Publication Data
Levitin, Sonia, 1934-
Adam's war / by Sonia Levitin;
pictures by Vincent Nasta
p.   cm.
Summary: When Adam and his friends start a war with a rival
club over a clubhouse, the conflict ends in violence.
ISBN 0-8037-1506-4 (trade).—ISBN 0-8037-1507-2 (library)
[1. Clubs—Fiction. 2. Violence—Fiction.] I. Nasta, Vincent, ill.
II. Title.
PZ7.L58Ad   1994   [Fic]—dc20   93-13833   CIP   AC

For Toni Mendez,
agent and friend
S . L .

For K.N., with love
V. N .

Contents

ONE

Adam's Find

Adam was up early, doing his chores. It was his job to empty the dishwasher and make lunches for himself and his mom, while his dad fixed breakfast.

Adam's dad smiled. "You're a good organizer, Son." He reached into his pocket, plucked out a quarter, and gave it to Adam. "Remember to take out the trash for your mom," he said.

Adam's mom worked at the junior high school office. She was always in a hurry to get there. She kissed Adam lightly on the cheek. "Good-bye, darling. Don't forget your key. Don't open the door to anyone. And no guests until I get home, understand?"

"Aw, Mom," said Adam, "can't I even have the guys from the club?"

"You know the rule, Adam."

"How can I keep a club going if we don't have a place to meet?" Adam complained.

"Adam, I don't have time for this," his mother said firmly.

"Why not meet at Hector's or Brendan's house?" his dad suggested. "Or you could play at the park."

"Hector's sisters are always screaming at him," Adam said. "Brendan lives too far away."

"What about the park?" his dad insisted.

"There's a bunch of little kids there and weird people sitting on the benches," Adam said.

His mom turned back. "Weird people? What do you mean, Adam?"

"Oh, nothing."

"I want to know!"

"Oh, just this old guy. Wears an army cap. He sits on the bench talking to himself all the time. It gives me the creeps."

"Well, just stay away from him," Adam's mother said. "Now, let's get out of here, or we'll all be late."

Adam ran the two blocks to Hector's house. He banged on the door. From inside came shrill rock music. "Hector! Come on!" Adam shouted.

Hector stumbled out, untidy and breathless. With four sisters, he got hardly any time in the bathroom. "Hector the Heckler" they called him, and they yelled at him, "Hector, get out, get out!"

Hector nearly tripped down the stairs. He buttoned up his shirt as they walked.

Adam walked fast; the mornings were getting cold. He zipped up his jacket. Last week the boys had talked about getting patches for their jackets, with their club name, ANGELS, stitched in black.

Everyone thought that was a great idea, but nobody knew where to get the patches. Hector had said he'd ask his sister Mary Beth who worked downtown. "Did you ask Mary Beth about our patches?" Adam asked him now.

Hector grunted. "Mary Beth isn't around much, and when she is, she doesn't talk to me."

"You said you'd ask her!" Adam wanted to grab Hector and give him a shake. "Can't you just ask her?"

"OK, OK. Leave me alone," muttered Hector, walking ahead. "I'm sick of you bugging me," he added.

"I'm sorry," Adam said, stepping up beside Hector. "I'm just thinking about the club. If we have patches, other guys will notice us and want to join. We need a few more members."

"Yeah, I guess," said Hector.

Adam walked briskly, and he tried to sound peppy. "We better have a meeting today," he said. "We can have it at my house after four-thirty. OK?"

"I guess," said Hector. "But we never do anything. I'm tired of just hanging around."

"I've got tons of plans," said Adam. He bit his lip; he didn't have any real plans. They had tried a baseball game with the Terrestrials, their rivals. It had ended in a fight. Once they had a cookout in Mike's backyard. A spark had landed on the garage roof and nearly started a fire. Brendan, their fourth member, invited them all to his violin recital, but that was no fun. The club seemed to be falling apart.

"This is a stupid club," Hector grumbled. "You said we'd have real neat adventures. This club stinks."

Adam wanted to yell at Hector, but he only walked along, thinking. It was very hard to keep things going. A leader always needed new ideas. That's what his dad said. "You've got to keep everyone motivated."

Motivated—that meant getting people to do things even if at first they didn't want to. His dad did that at the supermarket, where he was the manager.

Adam tried to sound excited. "Hey, maybe we could rent a video. Something really neat. We could make popcorn. Saturday, we could go hiking at Drew Canyon."

"Aw, who wants to take a dumb hike?" Hector muttered. He kicked a can right into the path of a fast-moving car. A moment later Hector ran to get the flattened can. He showed Adam.

"Neat-o," Adam said, pretending this was something great.

They approached the corner of Pilgrim Park. It was a small park, one city block, surrounded by a low iron fence. Now it was empty. Later, little kids would come with their baby-sitters and use the swings and the sandbox. The old veteran would sit on the bench with his dog beside him. Some days he sat for hours in a patch of sun, as if he was cold and could never get warm again.

Now Hector reminded Adam. "You said you'd talk to that creepy guy about letting us use his dog for a mascot."

"It would be great to have a mascot," Adam agreed. The dog was a beautiful husky.

"We could ask him," Hector continued. "I know he lives at the old soldier's home on Colton Street."

"Everyone knows that," Adam scoffed.

"Well, let's ask him, then," said Hector, tossing away his flattened can.

"Would you go with me?" Adam asked sharply.

"No way," said Hector.

Adam felt a rush of anger. He had, in fact, gone to Colton Street last week. He had felt breathless as he walked over to the dilapidated building with the peeling paint and the torn awnings. Several windows were broken and patched with plywood. Suddenly a burly man wearing a stained white shirt and pants came rushing out, shouting, "What in blazes are you hanging around here for? You want me to call the cops? Get outa here, we've had trouble enough with punks like you!" The man shook his fist, while his eyes blazed viciously at Adam.

Adam had run all the way back to his street, without ever seeing the veteran and his dog. Now Adam felt the anger all over again. Why were people so mean? And how could a creepy man like that old veteran have such a beautiful dog? It wasn't fair. "Next time we see him at the park," Adam decided, "I'll ask him."

"Sure, sure," said Hector with a grin.

As they passed Pilgrim Park, Adam noticed that the leaves were falling and the ground had that stiff look, preparing for winter.

Suddenly Adam gasped. "Hey!" he yelled. "Look at that! Wow! Come on!" He ran, hearing Hector's footsteps pounding on the pavement behind him, and he was filled with joy.

There, right in front of him, stood the answer to all his problems. Someone had built a shack in front of the tall dumpster. It seemed to have appeared, like magic, under the crooked maple tree.

Adam looked and looked. Hector stood beside him, panting.

"Neat-o!" Adam whispered. The walls of the shack were made of plywood and branches, cardboard and cloth, a few oddly shaped bits of metal, all pieced together. Part of an old blanket, flung back over the doorway, showed that the place was empty.

Adam turned to Hector. "What a great clubhouse for the Angels!" he exclaimed.

Adam watched Hector's face, as that bored look changed to excitement and admiration. "Yeah!" Hector cried. "Yeah!"

Angel Territory

The Angels always ate lunch together under one of the sycamore trees by the baseball field. This was Angel Territory. Today they had something to talk about.

Adam and Hector told Mike and Brendan about finding the clubhouse.

"Probably some homeless person made it to sleep in," said Brendan. "But where would he find all that stuff? And why wouldn't he still be in it?"

Mike smiled and his face lit up. "Maybe he makes houses all over the city and leaves 'em for other people. Maybe he's just a good guy."

Adam smiled. It was like Mike to think of such a thing. Mike thought everybody was nice.

"So, we've got ourselves a clubhouse," said Adam.

"Angel territory," echoed Hector. "Nobody else allowed." He stuck out his chin, looking tough.

"That's right," said Adam. "We'll go down there after school and clean it out."

"We can get a broom from my house," Hector said.

"I already wrote our club name on the side wall," Adam said. "Lucky I had a good marker on me."

"Did you put all our names?" Brendan asked. String-bean Brendan, they sometimes called him. Now Brendan stretched, making himself look even taller and skinnier. "You should have put all our names," he said.

"I figured we'd each write our own," Adam said.

"That would be better," Mike agreed. He always agreed. Even the Terrestrials liked Mike. They had asked him to join their group. But Mike didn't. He liked Adam and the Angels better.

"Those Terrestrials are big," Mike often said, "but they're dumb."

"Yeah," everyone agreed. "Big and dumb. Especially that Carl. He doesn't have all his marbles."

Carl was in Adam's PE class. Carl never followed directions, but the coach didn't seem to care, because Carl could jump hurdles better than anyone.

Now Adam asked, "Do you guys have any furniture we could put into our clubhouse?" He leaned against the fence, and the Angels surrounded him. Adam remembered to ask the others what they thought; that was important. "Maybe you guys have some ideas about fixing up the place."

"My mom has a little braided rug in the basement," Brendan said. "We could probably have it."

"Great idea," Adam said.

"We could bring chairs," said Hector.

"Or pillows," suggested Mike. "That might be better."

"Let's take a vote," Adam said. He felt very tall as he asked for a vote, and all the guys yelled, "Aye!" for the pillows, so it was settled.

"We'll get there right after school today," Adam said.

The bell rang. Kids started running toward the building.

"Aw, no!" Brendan moaned. "I can't. I've got a lesson today."

"I almost forgot," said Mike. "I've got karate."

Adam looked at his friends, his club. What did it take to get them together?

"Look, we need a meeting," Adam said seriously. "The Terrestrials are looking around for new members. If we don't get with it, they'll take all the best guys, like that new boy, Jamie Rand."

Adam spoke loudly. "We'll meet tomorrow for sure in our new clubhouse. I'll bring refreshments."

Brendan sounded skeptical. "Who pays?"

"I've got some money," Adam said. He had about three dollars saved. He'd spend it gladly for the club. He said, "We'll go right after school."

The boys agreed and started to leave.

"Wait!" Adam shouted. He held out his right hand, the palm down, first two fingers crossed and the others spread, their club sign.

Each boy laid his right hand on top of the others, then his left.

Adam felt the weight of all the boys' hands over his, and finally he placed his left hand over all the others, holding them together.

"OK," Adam said. "Remember." The boys all looked at him expectantly. "Pilgrim Park, right after school tomorrow," he said firmly. "We'll have doughnuts. But if you don't come, you're not going to be in the club, understand?"

"Yeah," said Hector. "Anybody doesn't show, they're out."

"We'll be there," said Mike cheerfully. "Hey, Adam,

this is really neat. I can't wait to see our clubhouse."

"This is gonna be great," Brendan said.

All afternoon while he sat in class, Adam dreamed about the clubhouse. They'd have cushions to sit on, maybe find a table. They'd have regular meetings. Adam thought he might buy a gavel to call the meetings to order. He'd seen that plenty of times on television.

Adam pictured having a bigger club, with eight or nine members. They'd always find great things to do. Maybe they'd even have a project, something good for the neighborhood, like collecting and taking in bottles and aluminum cans. Maybe their pictures would be in the paper, with the headline, ANGELS HELP CITY CLEANUP. Best of all, if anybody tried to pick on one of them, they'd stick together.

"Loyalty, that's what counts," Adam's dad always said. "Sticking together, like me and my pals in the navy. They were a great bunch of guys."

When you have a club, Adam thought, you're never alone. Maybe if he had a brother or even some sisters, Adam thought, he wouldn't care so much about the club. For years and years he'd hoped for a brother. None came.

He remembered how he got the idea of starting a club. It was last spring. About six guys he knew from school were on the playground, fooling around, shooting baskets. They all wore identical dark green

T-shirts. They had special names for one another like "Bonkie" and "Flip" and "Zulu." One of them, Steve Viccar, used to live down the street from Adam. Steve, turning from his buddies, called out to Adam and gave him a grin.

Watching them, Adam had wished more than anything that they might ask him to join. But, of course, they never would. They were all a year or two older than he. Besides, he wasn't an ace at basketball or anything. He did have friends, though. His mom always said, "People like Adam. He's a born leader." So he began to dream about starting a club of his own.

His dad thought it was a great idea. He gave Adam a little punch on the arm and said, "Way to go!"

Now Adam turned, realizing he was almost the last person out on the school yard. He ran across the blacktop and took a high, long leap over a couple of benches, as if he were flying.

The next afternoon the Angels marched toward Pilgrim Park. Adam carried a sack of doughnuts. They smelled sweet and tempting.

The four Angels took up the whole sidewalk. As they went, they sang their club song, to the tune of "One Hundred Bottles of Beer on the Wall." They made up new verses on the spot. The song had been

Brendan's idea. He started with their very first verse:

"Four Angels walking along,
Four Angel guys,
If we find another one singing this song,
Then there will be five!"

Laughing, the boys ran the rest of the way into the park, with Adam in the lead. He felt terrific.

The maple leaves were starting to turn. Little kids swung high on the swings. The veteran sat on the bench, nodding and muttering, his beautiful gray husky at his feet.

Adam glanced at the man and the dog; he wanted to speak but decided to wait until later. Later, maybe, the veteran would let the dog come into the club-house. Adam would share his doughnut with the husky. He could imagine the dog licking his fingers, and Adam would get down close beside the warm, furry body.

Adam had wanted a dog for ages, but there were always reasons against it. "It wouldn't be fair to the dog," said his mom. "We're always working." Besides, Adam's dad had allergies.

As Adam approached the shack, he looked for the word ANGELS that he had written with his black marker on the plywood. It was still there but ruined. Someone had smeared it with black paint and red jagged lines, dripping down like blood. Underneath the word ANGELS someone had written the word STINKS.

Adam moved closer. He heard a faint sound, a cough or a groan.

Quickly Adam jerked aside the cloth. There, at a low table, sat five boys, all grinning—the Terrestrials.

THREE

The Invaders

For a moment Adam could hardly get his breath. Then things came into focus, like a Polaroid picture gradually taking on shape and color.

The Terrestrials had moved in and taken over his clubhouse. Adam could hardly believe it.

"Hey," came a voice, loud and sassy. "I didn't hear you knock. Where's your manners?" There were jeers and laughter.

"Look at the little Angels!" called Troy, the Terrestrials' leader. "Ain't they sweet?"

Troy's elbows were propped on the low table. He had full lips and green eyes, the color of bottle glass. Troy never really smiled, but he never really stopped smiling either.

"Get out of our clubhouse," yelled Troy's buddy, Wes.

"Get out or we'll push you out," said Arlo. His arms were thick from pumping weights; Arlo had a big brother who worked at a gym.

The other two, Carl and Jerry, sat there grinning, fooling with a radio on the table. Suddenly it blasted out a rap song. Carl and Jerry yelled and banged their fists on the tabletop.

"Shut up," Troy shouted.

They did.

"You." Troy pointed at Adam. "Take your little sissy Angels and get out of here. We don't like the way you stink up our place. Carl, we don't want those guys in here," Troy said.

Carl stood up and rubbed his fist in his hand, grinning.

Adam turned. His buddies were waiting. Their breathing was heavy, from running and from the shock of seeing the invaders. Now they expected him to act.

"Look," Adam said. "This is our place. I saw it first."

"Ha!" laughed the Terrestrials, and they stamped their feet and whistled. "Who cares? It's ours now."

"No, it isn't," said Adam. "Finders keepers."

"Losers weepers!" screamed the Terrestrials.

"I found this shack two days ago," Adam said.

"Well, we've got it now," Troy said, and Wes echoed, "Yeah, we're holding a meeting."

Adam crossed his arms over his chest and stood his ground, then he put one foot inside the doorway. He kept his voice reasonable, talking slowly, the way his mother did when she got into an argument about car repairs or somebody charging her a wrong price.

Adam said, "Troy, the day before yesterday I wrote our name on the wall. That means this place belongs to us. If you want a clubhouse, you can build yourselves one over by the baseball diamond. There's a pile of wood and stuff across the street."

"We *have* our own house," said Troy with a steady gaze. "And we don't need any ideas from you. Now, get out before I push your face in."

"It's ours," Adam shouted. Hot anger swept over him; his heart pounded. His fists felt large and powerful, ready to destroy something, to prove his claim.

"You put your other foot in here," Troy threatened, "and we'll waste you."

Quickly Adam thought. Five Terrestrials, four Angels; they'd get beaten up. Ideas wavered in his mind, whether to stay or leave, fight or turn away, cowards.

Still looking at Troy, Adam shrugged and told his friends, "Let's go."

For an instant nobody moved. The three boys behind Adam were silent, but he could feel their resentment, almost like a wave of heat.

Adam glanced back at his friends. He gave them a nod, then turned to Troy and the other Terrestrials. "We're leaving now," Adam said, "but we'll be back. And then if you guys are still here, we'll pulverize you."

Troy stood up. All the Terrestrials stood beside him. "Try it," Troy said. "Just try it. You guys are too chicken to do anything."

"We're not scared of you!" Hector screamed out. "Just wait! We'll nail you guys!"

"Oh, oh, I'm so scared of Mama's little Angels!" Wes yelled. Arlo moved toward the doorway, with Carl and Jerry after him.

Adam backed up outside the hut. Troy and the others pressed closer.

Adam felt better out in the open, with his buddies close around him. "Look, Troy," he shouted, "I wrote our name on the wall. You must have heard us talking about this place at school. You stole it."

"What if we did?" Troy retorted. "Anyhow, you didn't build this hut. It doesn't belong to you."

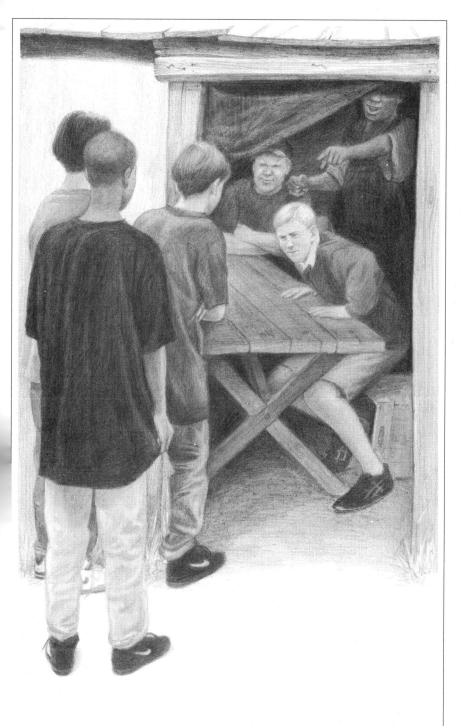

"It probably belongs to some homeless person," Brendan tried to explain.

"Well, I guess he's still homeless," laughed Troy. "Hey! Why don't you guys clean out that dumpster and meet in there? There's plenty of room in that dumpster for four wimps like you!"

The Terrestrials howled with laughter, and they kicked at the ground, doubled over.

"You think you're funny," Adam sputtered. Hatred made his mind go absolutely blank.

Suddenly he felt Troy's hands on his back, pushing him hard. "Get out," said Troy, low in his throat, threatening.

"Get your hands off me!" cried Adam.

Troy pushed Adam again, harder. Adam nearly tripped. His hand scraped painfully across the gravel. The sack of doughnuts fell to the ground.

Troy scooped it up. He dug in, pulled out the doughnuts one by one and tossed them to the Terrestrials. Doughnuts sailed through the air. A doughnut hit Arlo in the chest. He laughed and mashed it under his feet. Adam felt sick with anger.

Carl stuffed a jelly doughnut into his mouth. "Thanks for the eats!" he cried.

The rest of the doughnuts disappeared, trashed or eaten. Then the Terrestrials, full of energy, shrieked and hollered like warriors.

"Let's go, Adam," said Mike, sounding scared.

"We'll be back," screamed Hector as he started to run.

"Sure, sure," scoffed the Terrestrials.

Adam turned, not quite running. Someone threw a rock. It hit Adam on the leg. He felt the sting but pretended it hadn't even hurt. "Come on, Adam!" yelled Mike.

Another rock sailed past, this time near Adam's head. He ran.

Mike, Brendan, and Hector were half a block ahead of Adam. He wanted to scream for them to wait, but he couldn't. He was too angry, too ashamed. He'd let Troy push him around. Maybe the guys were calling him chicken. Some leader! A leader was supposed to be tough. He hadn't even defended himself. Adam wished he'd never seen that shack.

As they neared the corner, something made Adam turn. There was the veteran with his husky on the leash. The large dog stepped eagerly, his head erect and eyes bright. He moved like a young dog, well trained and willing.

Adam turned and ran toward the man and the dog. "Mister! Mister!" he called.

The veteran paused, squinting at Adam in surprise, as if nobody had spoken with him for a long, long time. His clothes clung to his lean body; the army cap was straight on his head.

Adam noticed for the first time that the veteran's

face was very thin, his ears large and dragging downward. But it was the man's eyes that held Adam speechless. They were a watery brown, like the bottom of a pond, and deep.

The man made a sound, less than a word.

"I wondered," Adam said, his heart pounding so that he felt each blow distinctly, "I like your dog. It's a beautiful dog."

"Yes," said the veteran, and the way he nodded his head reminded Adam of a leaf bobbing in the wind.

"We have a club," Adam said. "Maybe your dog would like to play with us. We'd take real good care of him. He could be—you know—our mascot."

The veteran looked at Adam, unblinking, and his mouth formed a dry round hole as he clearly said the word *no*.

Adam was speechless. Suddenly the dog sat up very straight and lifted his paw, placing it lightly against Adam's leg.

The veteran yanked the leash. "Heel, General!" he said, and turned up the street. The dog trotted obediently along.

Adam felt the sting of disappointment, almost like a blow. But in the next moment he realized that the other boys had been watching him, and they now came running toward him in disbelief. The boys surrounded Adam, all speaking at once.

"Wow! Did you really talk to the old guy? The dog

wanted to shake your hand. What'd he say? Did you ask him?"

"He said no," Adam told them.

"No? Bummer!" they all cried.

"Maybe if I ask him again," said Adam. "Maybe after he gets used to the idea."

"Aw, he'll never let us have the dog," Hector complained. "We don't have anything, and now . . ."

"Now we need to make some plans," Adam said firmly. He crossed his arms over his chest.

"What plans?" asked Brendan. He and Mike seemed ready to walk away.

"Battle plans," Adam said. "We can't let the Terrestrials get away with this. They'll think we're just sissies. I said we'd be back. I meant it."

The boys turned to face Adam again.

"Well, what can we do about it?" asked Brendan.

"Plenty," said Adam. "We're going to have a war."

FOUR

Snakes and Mice

It was too early to go to Adam's house. His mom wouldn't be home yet. "Let's go to your house," he told Hector.

"My sisters are there," Hector objected. "They're always finding work for me to do."

"We'll go out on your back porch," Adam said. "You can show us your snakes."

"OK," said Hector, and he led the way.

Hector had three pet snakes. They lived in a large

cage in the laundry room, crowded onto a shelf above the washer and drier.

As the boys walked along, four abreast on the sidewalk, Mike said, "Maybe we should just forget the clubhouse. Maybe we can meet at my place. I'll ask my folks."

"You already asked," Adam reminded him. "They said no. And your mom gets home even later than mine. We can't meet at night. My folks won't let me out."

Hector said stoutly, "We could have creamed 'em."

"No way," said Brendan.

"It was four against five," Adam said. "Arlo and Carl are bigger than any of us."

"And in better shape," added Mike. "I think we were right to leave." He asked Adam. "Are we really going to have a war?"

Adam drew the boys into a circle. He gazed at them and nodded soberly. "We have to," he said. "Otherwise everyone at school will hear about it and think we're chicken."

The other boys all nodded. "Yeah. We have to."

"When do we fight them?" Hector asked. He stood with his fists braced against his hips.

"We need to plan this," Adam said. "We need to really think about it and have a strategy."

"What's that?" Hector asked.

"A plan," said Brendan. "Like in a real war."

"So, how will we do it?" Mike asked.

"Maybe we could get rid of one or two of them," Brendan said. "You know, get them in trouble so they have to stay after school, then we can beat up the other three easy."

Adam nodded. "That's a good idea. But how do we get them in trouble without getting ourselves in trouble?"

"You're the chief," Hector said with a laugh. "You tell us."

They had come to Hector's front door. "Shh!" Hector put his finger to his lips. Carefully he un-locked the door, and everyone tiptoed in after him. From the bedroom came the blast of a stereo and the sound of giggling.

Stepping lightly, the boys hurried through the house after Hector and to the tiny laundry room.

With the washer and drier, there was hardly space for the boys to stand. Hector opened the door. Mike and Brendan stepped out onto the small back porch. Mike sat down on the lower step, looking over his shoulder.

"Want to see 'em?" Hector asked. He lifted the cage off the shelf. Inside were three snakes, two coiled, one waving about, looking for food. They were brown and pale green, nonpoisonous, but their bodies were thick and their eyes glittered brightly.

"I don't like snakes," Mike said.

Hector reached in and brought out the largest of the snakes. It was more than two feet long, and it wound itself around Hector's neck, coiling its tail around Hector's arm.

Brendan edged away, pressing against the porch railing.

"You guys are sissies," Hector said. "Hey! I've got a great idea. Know what we can do? We can take these snakes over to the park and put them in that hut and . . ."

Instantly Adam caught on, and with a laugh he cried out, "Yeah! That'll sure make the Terrestrials move!"

"Yeah!" all the boys shouted, leaping up and down until a girl's voice called out, "Hector, is that you? You're supposed to sweep out the basement this afternoon!"

Hector stood absolutely still. "Shh," he whispered, stifling a giggle. "Listen, maybe we could find some more snakes and put a whole bunch of them in that clubhouse. I'd love to see those Terrestrials screaming and running away! Then, when they're gone, we'll wreck down the hut, maybe even set it on fire."

"What a stupid idea!" Brendan objected. "If we wreck it, how can we use it?"

"Wait," said Adam. "What about your snakes? How will you get them back?"

"Simple," said Hector. "I'll bait them."

"With what?" asked Mike.

"Food."

"What do they eat?" Adam asked.

Hector grinned. "I'll show you. In fact, it's feeding time today. This guy eats only every couple of weeks. But when he does, it's neat-o."

Something in Hector's tone made Adam feel odd, almost chilled. "I thought you just feed them hamburger," Adam said. "What's so neat about seeing a snake eat hamburger?"

"We decided to change their diet," said Hector with a laugh. "Snakes like to hunt their food. They like mice. My dad got me some mousetraps. But my sister Ilene stuck her finger in one of them, so we decided to buy our own mice and raise them."

Hector bent down and opened a narrow cupboard beside the washer. Instantly the tiny room was filled with squeaking sounds as Hector lifted out a cage containing five or six small mice. They raced around the cage, noisy and panicked.

"We're breeding them," Hector explained. "See this one?" He pointed to a fat mouse squatting in a corner, eating out of a dish fastened to the bars. "It's pregnant," he said.

"You're going to feed the babies to the snakes?" Mike exclaimed, aghast.

"Sure," said Hector. "That's what we're raising them for."

"Hector!" shouted Adam. "That's so mean!"

"It is not," Hector objected. "It's just normal. Snakes eat mice. What's the difference whether I raise them or not? Hamburger is meat too. It used to be a cow."

"Shut up," said Mike.

"It's the truth!" shouted Hector.

"What are you going to do?" asked Adam, staring, for Hector had pulled one of the mice out of the cage and now he held it tightly in his hand. With his other hand Hector uncoiled the snake from around his shoulders and set it down on top of the washer.

The snake lay motionless on the cold surface, watching Hector intently.

"He knows," Hector whispered. "Come on."

Breathless, Adam drew closer. Mike and Brendan too crowded into the small room.

Adam saw the flush on Hector's face. His own breathing was rapid, both from dread and excitement. Somehow he felt as if he were seeing a thriller on television. Though it made him feel sick, he had to keep watching.

Hector opened his hand.

The mouse squatted on the white metal surface of the washer, paralyzed. Then with a cry it leapt.

The snake struck.

It was over in an instant. Adam saw the flash of the snake's jaws open wide, then the bulging movement along the snake's throat as the mouse slid down.

"Gross," Adam moaned. He thought he was going to be sick.

The snake lay limp for a moment, then arched itself and gave a slight shudder.

"Put it back," Adam said gruffly.

Hector pushed the snake back into the cage. Everyone sat down on the porch steps. Adam felt suddenly tired, as if he'd played nine innings of baseball or gone bike riding for miles and miles. He wasn't even hungry for dinner, nor did he feel like talking and making any plans.

"Hector, you're a creep!" Brendan burst out.

Mike looked ready to cry.

"Who're you calling a creep?" Hector yelled, making a fist.

"Cut it out, guys," said Adam. "Hector didn't mean anything. It's his mouse. His snake."

"I don't think I want to stay here," said Brendan, getting up to leave.

"Sit down," said Adam. "We've got to have this meeting. Look, it's the Terrestrials we're mad at. The

Terrible Terrestrials. They beat up on people. They steal. They're selfish and mean. Now, let's get this meeting started."

Brendan sighed, stretched, and he sat back down on the bottom step. "OK," he said. "When's this big war going to happen?"

"Will we bring the snakes?" Mike asked. His voice shook and he looked pale.

"No," said Adam. He couldn't stand the thought of it, even though he didn't particularly like snakes. It just seemed wrong. But he didn't say that. Instead Adam told them, "We have to fight the regular way, with our fists. Otherwise they'll say we fight dirty."

Adam was feeling a little better now, taking charge. He added, "We could scare 'em, though, by making noise or something."

Mike said, "We could get those big coffee cans and fill them up with rocks and throw them."

"I have some firecrackers left over from Fourth of July," said Hector. "We could set those off—scare the pants off them!"

"Yeah!" yelled the boys, and Hector jumped up and down.

"So, after we scare them," said Adam, "we each take one. Brendan, who do you want to take?"

"I'll take Wes. He's about my size," Brendan said, stretching out his fingers.

"I'll take Arlo," said Mike. "I can use my karate as long as it's in self-defense."

"Hector can take Jerry," Adam said. "I'll take Troy."

Everyone nodded. The leader has to take the leader.

"What about Carl?" Mike asked.

"That's the problem," Adam said, biting his lip. "Carl's so big. He must weigh a hundred and thirty pounds."

"We need another member," Brendan said. "Then it would at least be even."

"Right," Adam said. "We have to get another Angel. We have to find one soon. Maybe tomorrow."

"When's this war going to start?" asked Mike.

Adam thought carefully, then replied, "Saturday. The Terrestrials always hang out together on Saturdays. For sure, they'll want to use the clubhouse, probably try to fix it up. So," Adam said, squinting, "we'll attack on Saturday. Maybe you guys can all sleep over Friday night. We'll get to the park early, real early. We'll wait inside the clubhouse. Then, when they come, we'll blast them."

Everyone nodded in agreement.

"Who can we get for the new member?" the boys all asked, waiting for Adam to decide.

"What about Jamie Rand?" Adam suggested. "He

sits beside me in class. He's cool. Do you want me to ask him? All in favor?"

"Aye!" everyone said, cheering.

"OK," said Adam. "We'll talk to Jamie tomorrow."

The next day, as Adam approached his classroom, Jamie Rand stood outside, talking to Troy.

"We're getting real neat sweatshirts," Troy was saying. "My dad got 'em for us. He got eight, so we can take in three more members. And we've got a clubhouse and everything. Want to join?"

Adam turned away, disgusted. Jamie and Troy were so engrossed, they didn't even notice him.

Adam saw Greg Huff walking by. Greg never said much, but he was a good soccer player. That meant that in a fight he'd have a powerful kick.

"Hey, Greg!" Adam called, smiling warmly. "How's it going?"

But he felt a little guilty. He'd hardly even talked to Greg before. Greg had a habit of shouting when he spoke, and he'd move in close, as if he was going to land a punch. Adam had never really wanted to be friends with Greg. On the other hand, if they were going to have a war, they needed someone like Greg Huff.

Adam went up to Greg and said, "Hey, I saw you playing soccer the other day. You've got a great kick.

Maybe if I practice, I could try out for the team next year."

"Sure," shouted Greg, grinning happily. "Any time."

Adam gave Greg a short, friendly jab and a nod, as if they were already pals.

FIVE

The First Fight

While the teacher was writing on the chalkboard, her back turned to the class, Adam whispered to Jamie.

"I saw you and Troy out in the hall," he began.

Jamie nodded. "He asked me to join their club."

"The Terrestrials," said Adam. "Do you like those guys?"

"I don't know them very well," Jamie said. "What are they like?"

Adam made a face. "Wes and Jerry are OK, I guess,

but that Carl—he's nuts. And Arlo's just a big moose."

Jamie looked doubtful. Quickly Adam said, "I guess Troy's OK too."

Jamie said, "Troy told me they're getting sweatshirts and everything. Troy said his dad is going to take all the guys to the mountains in his truck next spring."

"Spring is a long time away," remarked Adam. "I've got a club too, you know."

"I know," Jamie whispered. "Angels."

"Our guys are really neat. Brendan plays in the orchestra, he's real tall and skinny. Hector's my best friend. He lives close by. Mike is . . ."

"I know Mike. I like him."

"We were thinking," Adam said, "you might want to join the Angels. We talked about it yesterday."

Jamie looked worried. "The Terrestrials asked me first," he said with a frown.

"But don't you think you should be with the guys you like the best?"

"Troy thinks I'm going to join the Terrestrials," said Jamie. He glanced about, then whispered to Adam, "He already told me things about the club. They have a secret password. And they've got a mascot."

"They do? What is it?"

"A tortoise."

"Ha! What a dumb mascot!" Adam exclaimed. The teacher turned, frowning, then continued to write on the chalkboard.

Adam whispered to Jamie, "We've got a dog, a beautiful, big dog, a husky. He belongs to a friend of ours, a guy who was a general."

"A general in the army?" asked Jamie, impressed.

"Yeah. And this dog, you should see it, it does everything he tells it. It does what I tell it too. And when we go on an overnight, we'll take the dog along. Maybe we'll even rent some horses. You like to ride horses?"

"Sure. But I've ridden only a couple of times," said Jamie.

"That doesn't matter. Brendan's a real good rider. He'll help you. He's a great guy."

The teacher turned, clapped her hands together, and called out, "No talking!"

Adam breathed a sigh of relief. He'd been getting carried away. Hearing that word *mascot* had really jolted him. It wasn't actually a lie about the dog. He'd talk to the veteran again as soon as he could.

Now Adam bent over his desk, trying to concentrate on the lesson. All he could think of was getting Jamie to join the Angels.

Adam bent close to Jamie. "The Angels always eat

together," he whispered. "Want to eat lunch with us today?"

Jamie nodded, smiling broadly.

"Adam! Jamie!" the teacher scolded. "*No talking.* Let's all keep our eyes on our own papers."

At lunchtime Adam walked out with Jamie. They hurried to Mike and Hector's classroom and caught up with them in the hall. Brendan, coming from orchestra practice in the auditorium, joined them.

The boys hurried out through the crowded halls. They sat on the benches under the sycamore tree, eating and laughing and fooling around. Jamie seemed to be having a good time. He and Mike really hit it off.

Adam waited awhile, then got down to business. "I asked Jamie to join the Angels," he said.

"All right," everyone said, and, "Way to go!"

Adam stood up, and he asked Jamie, "Do you want to join our club?"

Jamie paused, then he nodded happily and said, "Sure!"

The boys cheered and punched Jamie on the back. Adam waited for them to settle down. The Angels showed Jamie their club sign and club handshake. The boys stood in a circle, their hands outstretched in their secret handshake. Adam thought that they looked like a wheel, with all their hands together in the center. He felt so proud that he wished his dad were here, watching.

Then Adam told his friends the good news. "My mom said you can all sleep over Friday night."

"Great!" the boys all shouted. "Can we get a video?"

"Let's get a comedy," Mike said.

"Let's get something scary," said Hector.

"I can bring a video," Jamie offered. "My mom has stacks of them. I'll bring a few and you guys can choose."

Adam grinned. Jamie was going to be a terrific member, he could tell.

"You can all eat over too," Adam said. "We'll have hot dogs and potato chips. My mom said she'll make us s'mores in the oven for dessert."

"Do you think you can come, Jamie?" asked Mike.

"Well, I have to ask, but I think so." Jamie frowned. "We're going up to my sister's house in the country, and my mom likes to leave by nine."

The Angels looked at one another. Brendan shook his head. "We might not be done by then," he said stiffly.

"Done with what?" asked Jamie. He blew up his lunch bag, popped it loudly, and tossed it into the trash can.

"We've got a project," said Hector. He started to giggle.

"Shut up, Hector," Adam said tensely. It was a mistake but too late to take it back.

"Don't tell me to shut up!" Hector cried. "Don't ever tell me to shut up!"

"I'm sorry," Adam began, but Jamie turned to Mike and asked, "What's going on?"

Mike shrugged and rolled his eyes, then said, "Well, on Saturday we're having a little—uh—a meeting with the Terrestrials."

"Yeah, a meeting at the park!" shouted Hector. He jumped onto the bench and stood there making jabbing motions with his fists. "They stole our clubhouse. We're having a war."

Jamie was biting his lip, looking upset. "I don't know," he said. "I need to be home early."

Adam began to sweat. He wished Hector would learn to keep his mouth shut.

"It's true," Adam said, looking at Jamie. "The Terrestrials stole our clubhouse, and they want to fight us. We tried to talk to them. They wouldn't listen. They think they can just bully everyone and take whatever they want. We decided, we have to teach them a lesson."

"They punched Adam," Brendan added.

"There was five of them and four of us," said Hector. "They are dirty fighters."

"We have to defend ourselves," Mike said. "They started it."

Jamie's eyes flicked uneasily from one boy to the next. "I don't know," he said.

"What don't you know?" asked Adam. He leaned against the back of the bench, motioning for the others to give Jamie some space. "Look, you can do what you want. We're asking you to join us because we're going to have a great club. The best. And we all want you in it. Don't we?"

"Sure," said the boys. "We voted on it," added Mike.

"We're getting club jackets and everything," said Hector.

"Well, I know," said Jamie with a shrug, "but I'm just not sure I can come Friday."

"Mostly," Adam said, "we're just going to scare those guys."

"Yeah," said Hector. "We thought about bringing some snakes."

"Snakes!" Jamie cried, backing off.

"Hector, you idiot!" Adam shouted, beside himself. With effort, he lowered his voice and tried to calm down. "Don't you remember? We decided not to do that. We're just going to go on over there, maybe take the dog with us. . . ."

"What dog?" asked Mike.

"The—mascot," said Adam. "General." Adam gave Mike a warning glance, then turned to Jamie. "Look, it's not such a big deal. We'll be back at my house by eight. You can still get home early, Jamie. Besides, we don't really have to fight, I mean, not really. We just need to show 'em that we aren't scared."

Now, at a distance, Adam saw Troy and Wes watching them. Jamie turned and saw them too.

Jamie said quickly, "Hey, I'll see you guys later," and he took off.

Adam was furious. He turned to Hector. "Look what you've done."

"Me? I didn't do anything."

"You told him about our war!" Adam shouted. "You got him so scared, he doesn't even want to join."

"Well, who wants him? He's just a sissy, anyway," screamed Hector.

"We all wanted him!" yelled Adam, moving toward Hector, "and you wrecked it. You told him our plans. It was a secret."

"Nobody said it was a secret!" Hector exploded, swinging his fists. When Hector got mad, his hair seemed to stand on end.

Adam moved in closer. "Do you think people go around advertising a war?" he screamed. "How can you be so dumb?"

Hector turned, kicked out with his foot, and caught Adam in the shins. Instantly Adam's fists went up and out, and he hit Hector squarely in the mouth.

Blood spurted onto Adam's hand. He stared at the blood. Hector's lip started to swell. Then Adam felt a resounding blow against the side of his head and another on his eye. Adam reeled back and nearly fell. He found his balance. He swung again, and he heard a crack as his fist hit Hector's jaw.

"Break it up! Break it up!" several people shouted.

Adam felt himself being roughly pulled away. Strong hands gripped him tightly around the chest. It was the yard duty monitors, two boys from the high school.

"Break it up!" the monitors yelled. "Cut it out. You want to go to the principal's office?"

Still dazed, Adam shook his head. Tears stung his eyes. His nose felt numb. He kept his head down. He mustn't let the Angels see their leader crying.

SIX

Needed:
Another Angel

The monitors took Adam to the school nurse. She cleaned his face with something cool and soothing, and he didn't have to go back to class.

Adam laid down on a cot in the nurse's office. He fell asleep and awakened, sore. His face hurt under his eye. When the final bell rang, Adam waited until he thought Hector had left for home. Then he walked alone, slowly, running his tongue over his dry lips, imagining how Hector must feel. Maybe he'd even gotten a tooth knocked out.

Of course, Adam had had fights before, but not like this. He had never fought with a good friend or seen blood on his hands. It made him shiver.

When Adam's mom came home, she gasped. "Look at your eye! You've got a black eye!" She fussed over him and worried and scolded. She got him an ice pack and brought iodine for the cut on his hand. Then she made Adam tell her about the fight, and when she found out it was his friend Hector, she said, "You've got to make up."

"Let him make up with me," said Adam.

"No," said his mother. "You should be the one. You're the leader."

"He kicked me first."

"Friendship isn't about being first or even about being right," Adam's mom said. "It's about forgiving. You and Hector have been friends for two years. What started the fight, anyway?"

"Oh, nothing," said Adam, looking away. "Nothing much."

"Something must have started it," his mom insisted.

Adam stood up and said, "OK, Mom. I'll call Hector and tell him I'm sorry we got into a fight. I'll tell him we should still be friends."

Adam's mom came close, and she put her arm around him. "That's my boy," she said proudly.

At first Hector wouldn't even come to the phone. Finally, when he answered, Adam could tell that Hector had been crying.

"Hey," said Adam. "How's your mouth?"

"It's OK. How's your eye?"

"OK. Hey, Hector, no hard feelings?"

"No hard feelings," said Hector. "See you tomorrow. OK?"

"OK. I'll come by your house in the morning, early."

When Adam's dad came home, he too wanted to know all about the fight. "What happened?" he asked, looking closely at Adam's face. "That's quite a shiner. What'd the other guy look like?" He grinned.

Adam said. "He didn't lose a tooth or anything. We talked on the phone and made up."

"That's good, Son," said his dad.

"It would have been better not to fight in the first place," said Adam's mom.

"Now, Sylvia, that's unrealistic," said his dad.

"Violence never solved anything," insisted Adam's mom.

"That may be true," said Adam's dad. "But sometimes you have to fight. Sometimes there's no other way."

"People should learn to talk over their differences."

"Oh? Really? Then how come you're taking that course—self-defense for women. Aren't you learning to use force to protect yourself?"

"That's different," cried Adam's mom.

"It's not different!" exclaimed Adam's dad. "If someone tries to attack you, are you going to just sit down and talk about it? Or are you going to belt him one?"

"I don't want to discuss this further," said Adam's mom.

"You shouldn't," snapped Adam's father. "You don't know what you're talking about."

For the rest of the evening his parents sat in stiff, angry silence.

Adam went to his room. He wished he could ask his dad to help him figure out how to beat the Terrestrials. But he knew if he said anything, his mom would get on his case. No, he had to do this alone.

Late that night Adam's dad came in to see him. Adam was nearly asleep, but he sat up in bed and tried to smile. His lip hurt and so did his eye.

"How're you feeling, Son?" asked Adam's dad.

"OK, I guess," Adam said.

His dad sat down on Adam's bed. "What was that fight all about?"

"Hector kicked me," said Adam. "I just fought

back. Don't you think people have to fight back sometimes?"

His dad nodded. "Some people are born bullies. If they get away with being mean, it only makes them meaner. But Hector's not like that. Hector's your friend."

"We made up," Adam said.

"That's good. I'm glad. When I was a kid," his dad said thoughtfully, "I once had a big fight. My friend flattened me. After that we kept on hating each other all through school."

"What happened to him, Dad?" Adam asked.

"I sometimes wonder," said his dad. "We'd been good pals too." He sighed.

"But you had a lot of pals when you were in the navy," Adam said. "Wasn't that great?"

"Sure, parts of it were good," his dad replied, "like being together with the other guys, feeling that we were doing the right thing. But some of it was terrible."

"What was terrible, Dad?" Adam asked, although he thought he already knew.

"People got killed," said his father. "Some of our buddies got killed. That was terrible." He put his arm around Adam and drew him close.

"I know what you mean about bullies, Dad," Adam said. Now he told his father about the Terrestrials.

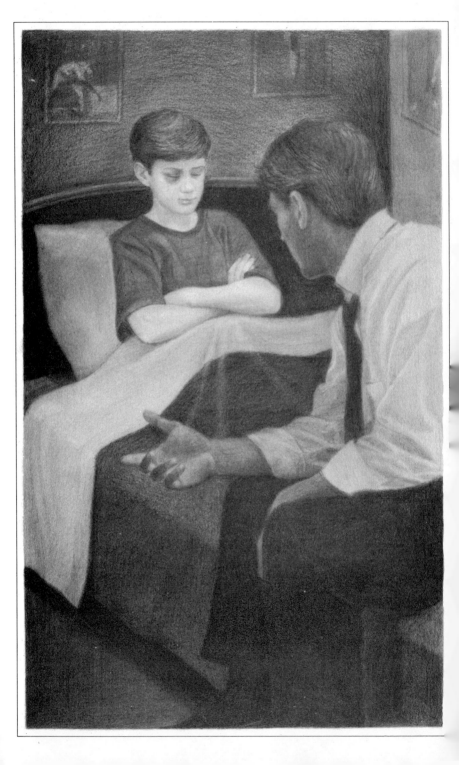

"We can't let them push us around, Dad," he said. "It's like you said. So, we're going to fight 'em."

Adam's father frowned. "Does your mother know about this?"

"No. I think she'd be mad."

"I think you're right, Son," said his father. "Look, I think you need to try to reason with people. But if you have to fight, all I can say is, be prepared. Be careful."

"There's five of them," said Adam, "and only four of us."

"Then give it up," said his dad, "or find yourself another member."

"Jamie was supposed to be the new member, but he couldn't decide." Adam pushed the covers aside and clenched his fists, remembering. "First Jamie said he'd go with the Terrestrials. Then he wanted to go with us. But Hector wrecked it. That's what really started the fight, Dad. Why couldn't Hector shut up? Why couldn't Jamie make up his mind?"

His dad smiled and patted Adam's shoulder. "It's tough being in charge, isn't it? You'll work it out," he added. "Sleep well, Son."

But Adam couldn't get to sleep for a long time.

Jamie wasn't at school the next day or the next. Adam didn't know where he lived, nor did he have his phone number.

"Maybe he's got a cold or something," Hector said.

"So, we can't count on him for Saturday," Hector said.

"We need another guy," said Hector, "or we're going to get creamed."

"We'd better have a meeting at lunchtime," said Adam.

When all the Angels were assembled under the sycamore tree, Adam laid out their choices. "Who do we know who would make a good Angel?" he asked.

The boys all shook their heads. They had been through this before. A lot of the boys lived too far away and came on the bus; they'd never be able to stay for afternoon or Saturday meetings.

"What about Greg Huff?" Brendan suggested.

"What about him?" scoffed Hector. "He's a pest."

"He's big," said Mike. "He plays soccer."

"I thought of him myself," said Adam. "Let's ask him."

"To join the Angels?" exclaimed Hector.

"Sure," said Adam. "Why not? He's OK."

Brendan stood up and stretched. "Maybe it's not enough just to be OK," he said. "We're going to be stuck with him for a long time."

"Maybe after the war," suggested Hector, "we can tell him to get lost."

Nobody said anything, and Adam too kept silent. Tell Greg to just get lost? It might not be that simple.

Adam felt the weight of being in charge. He couldn't figure out everything this minute; the most important thing was getting even with the Terrestrials.

Adam said, "Is it agreed, then? Should we ask Greg to join? I know he'll be able to come tonight. His folks are never around. He's always just hanging out at the store or the arcade."

"Ask him," said Mike. "We'll probably like him when we get to know him. He probably needs some friends."

Adam nodded and said, "OK. Let's find Greg. We can swear him in right now before the bell rings."

Finding Greg was easy. He was practicing with a soccer ball, kicking it against the gym wall. Getting him to join the Angels was easy too. The more the Angels talked, the brighter Greg's eyes became, and by the time they showed him their club sign and handshake, Greg was grinning like a jack-o'-lantern.

When Adam told Greg about the sleep-over, Greg kept shouting, "Sure, sure, I'll be there. I know where you live. I walk by your house all the time. Sometimes I see you outside. Hey, this is gonna be great. Really great."

Adam gave Greg a big smile, and he flashed the Angels' sign.

« S E V E N »

Set for Battle

Late Friday afternoon all the Angels came to Adam's house. They sat on the floor in Adam's room, and they got ready for the war.

They made banners that said ANGELS. Later they'd hang the banners in their clubhouse. Hector made a big skull and crossbones in black on a yellow piece of paper. It looked great. Mike drew an angel carrying a sword.

Brendan made up a new verse to their song, about

how they'd pulverize the Terrestrials and then anyone else who tried to fight them.

Greg learned the song and sang it over and over.
"Gee, I've never been in a club," he shouted. "This
is great." He wore cowboy boots, and he had brought
an old cap gun along. It was hooked into his belt.

"What's that for?" Hector laughed, pointing.
"We're not using baby toys, you know."

"Oh, I just brought it," Greg said.

"It's OK," said Adam. He laughed. "The Terrestrials are so dumb, maybe they'll think it's real."

Everyone laughed and laughed, and Adam found
a couple of old cap guns of his in the closet, and the
boys practiced drawing the pistols out of their belts,
like in the Westerns on TV.

They were having such a great time that Adam
was surprised when his mom called them all to sup-
per. She had laid everything out on the dining room
table—hot dogs, chips, pickles, carrots, and celery,
and a stack of chocolate bars, graham crackers, and
marshmallows for the s'mores.

As Adam saw his friends gathered around the table, this seemed like the best day of his life, even
better than a birthday. Everybody was having so
much fun. Adam's dad came home and turned on
the stereo, and his folks helped themselves to hot
dogs and sat down and talked with the boys.

Later they all went out and played Kick-the-Can. Greg had a terrific kick, and he could run fast. Adam's dad played too. Then, when it was getting dark, Adam's mom came to the door with a platter of hot, bubbling s'mores, and the guys ran in and they all sat down on the rug in the living room and ate the s'mores and told jokes.

As Adam looked around at all the Angels, the clubhouse didn't seem very important anymore. He thought about what they might do tomorrow morning, if they weren't having a war. They could go hiking or maybe even go horseback riding, if his dad would take them. Even if they hung around here, they could have a good time playing Kick-the-Can or Capture-the-Flag. They could go down to the park and hit baseballs.

When it was late, all the guys laid out their sleeping bags on the floor in Adam's room. It was crowded, but Adam loved having everyone there.

He sat on the bed, looking down at his friends. They were sleepy but still talking, making plans. Brendan had brought an old army belt of his dad's and a slingshot. His pockets were stuffed with pebbles. Hector had brought several books of matches to light the firecrackers. Mike, when he thought nobody was looking, took some lunges and chops, just to keep himself in shape.

"You guys," Adam suddenly said, "are you sure you want to go through with this war?"

The boys stared at him in amazement. "What's wrong with you?" Hector cried. "Are you chickening out on us?"

"They stole our clubhouse!" Greg yelled.

"We can't let them get away with it," said Mike. "Those guys are so nasty. I saw Troy and Wes picking on a little first grader yesterday; they pushed him and he got a bloody nose."

"We've got it all planned," said Hector. "We're getting up real early. We'll be in the clubhouse when they get there. We'll cream them!"

"We'll be the kings of the school!" said Greg.

"Right," said Adam. "Right. I was just checking."

But that night, while all the other boys slept, Adam lay awake. He heard their breathing in the darkness. He remembered something from when he was very little. He had gotten into his mom's car standing in the driveway.

He sat there turning the steering wheel, making motor noises in his throat. He felt big sitting in the driver's seat. He honked the horn, pretending he was on the freeway, and he pushed the blinker signal up, and he reached down and pulled the big handle toward him, the way he'd seen his mother do hundreds of times—and suddenly he heard a strange sound, a click, and then the car began to move faster, faster, faster, until it was speeding down the hill, headed straight for traffic.

Adam remembered the panic, the screams, his own, and then his mother's as she came running toward him. Her eyes looked wild, and she was screaming his name. "Adam! Adam!" Her hands seemed to fly toward him, but still the car sped away. The wheel spun out of Adam's grasp. The car was like a wild thing, taking off on its own, ready to crash.

Now Adam shivered. Something about the dark night and the thought of tomorrow morning was just like that car speeding down the hill, and he was unable to stop it.

Then his mother had managed to jump into the car and push Adam aside. She had stopped the car before it got into traffic on the main road. Adam's mother had sat there, her face in her hands, crying and crying. "Promise me you'll never do such a thing again!" she had sobbed.

Adam promised, and he had kept his word.

Now it wasn't so easy to keep all the many different promises he had made.

Adam lay very stiff and still. After a time he heard someone move, and he saw a tall, lanky figure creeping toward him.

"Adam?" Brendan whispered. "Are you awake?"

"Yeah." Adam sat up in his bed. Brendan sat down beside him, on the edge.

"Jerry plays the tuba in the orchestra," Brendan whispered.

"So?" whispered Adam.

"Yesterday he told me the Terrestrials can't wait to beat us up. He said we better stay out of Pilgrim Park, if we know what's good for us. I didn't want to tell the other guys. I figured, they'd be scared and then . . ."

"Jerry could just be bluffing," Adam said.

"That's what I thought," said Brendan, nodding. "Anyway, we've got a right to go to Pilgrim Park. It's a public park."

"They don't own it," Adam agreed.

"But, then," Brendan whispered, "there's another park on the other side of the school. Maybe we could meet there and let the Terrestrials just have Pilgrim Park."

"If we back down now," Adam said, "the club will fall apart. Hector and Greg want this war. They're excited. Anyhow, with Greg on our side we can't lose."

"Carl's awfully big," Brendan said doubtfully.

"Are you trying to back out?" Adam asked.

"No! No!" Brendan whispered harshly. "No way. I'm just—thinking. I don't want to hurt my hands.

If I bust my finger, how can I play the violin?"

"Brendan," Adam said firmly, "you have to. Do you want to be an Angel? Or do you want to be in the orchestra?"

"Both!"

"If you want to be in the club, you have to take some chances. You've got to do things for your friends. The most important thing is to stick together. Don't you remember our club handshake? Our promise?"

"Sure," said Brendan. "Hey, I didn't mean anything. You know what? I've got this terrific slingshot. I've been practicing. Yesterday I knocked a pear right out of a tree so hard, it broke in two."

"Great," said Adam. "Listen," he whispered, talking fast. "I figure, the Terrestrials might not even come to the park tomorrow. So, we get the clubhouse back without doing anything. Then, I thought, we might even decide to tear it down. That way the Terrestrials can't get it, and we don't have to fight for it, and we can just meet at school, like we did the other day."

"Then why are we having a war about the clubhouse?" asked Brendan, and he clasped his arms around himself.

"It's not about the clubhouse," Adam argued. "It's about not getting pushed around. It's like . . ." Adam paused. He rubbed his eyes; he felt very tired. He whispered, "If we beat the Terrestrials, we'll be heroes."

"Yeah, heroes," whispered Brendan, and Adam could see him smiling in the shadows.

EIGHT

The Spy

Adam heard the sounds of a great motor. He felt the wind against his face, almost blinding him. Out of the fog he heard a grinding noise, and he knew the engine had failed. He sat in the cockpit of a huge airplane, his hands grasping the steering wheel. Behind him voices rang out, "Watch it! Look out!"

He looked around for the pilot. Then Adam realized he was the pilot. All the passengers were counting on him to bring the plane in for a landing. Adam strained to see out the window. Fog and rain blurred everything. He turned the wheel and pulled it toward him. Suddenly the wheel came loose in his hands, and he felt himself being hurled downward faster and faster and faster, ready to crash.

Adam sat up with a jolt. His feet tingled; his arms ached. He heard someone snoring loudly. He felt weak.

"Pull yourself together," Adam said half aloud. It was what his dad always said in a crisis. "Pull yourself together."

Adam lay very still, telling himself there was no plane, no motor, nothing going out of control. He was here in his own bed, with all his friends around him. He smiled to himself. That awful sound of the airplane motor in his dream was nothing more than the snores from Greg, who slept with his mouth open on his back, sputtering like an engine.

It was eight-thirty in the morning. Adam had planned to get up early, but everyone overslept. Adam woke up first. He pulled the boys out of their sleeping bags and got everyone going.

The Angels ate a breakfast of oranges and dough-nuts and cocoa. Adam's mom went on her way to do the weekly shopping. She told the boys how good they'd been, and the Angels all said, "Thank you," and she said they could do it again sometime.

The boys ran outside, laughing and yelling and

having the best time ever. With Adam leading, they marched toward Pilgrim Park, moving fast.

Brendan had his pockets filled with stones.

Hector had a sack full of firecrackers.

Mike picked up a thick stick on the way.

Greg had his cap gun and his best weapon, his own feet, clad in boots.

Adam walked fast. He knew he could land a good, hard punch. The fight with Hector had proved that. He wasn't scared. In fact, now he felt very excited and happy. He wanted to wave at people in passing cars. Now and then he glanced back at the guys, and they grinned at him or gave him the OK sign.

Adam walked proudly. They were right to fight for their clubhouse. Only wimps let other people steal what is theirs. The Terrestrials were bullies. You can't let a bully get away with being mean, because he will only get meaner.

Besides, they were going to win. Adam felt it in his bones.

The sun was shining. A group of grown-ups on bikes rode past the Angels, waving. People were walking their dogs. A couple of little kids raced into Pilgrim Park and jumped onto the swings.

At the park entrance Adam called the guys into a huddle.

"This is going to be great," he said. "The Terrestrials will never know what hit them. Now, when we

get into the clubhouse, I want you guys all to stay
down and keep quiet. As soon as they come, we'll
rush them."

It was their only chance, a surprise attack.

Adam heard a rattling sound. He looked back at
Hector. "What are you going to do with that?"
Hector carried a thick rope, with a metal chain tied
to the end.

"This is for Carl," Hector said. "I'm going to swing
this at him and knock him out. Then we can get the
rest of them, easy."

Adam started to say something, but the other boys
all cheered and cried out, "Hey, way to go!" So Adam
said nothing. It's the Terrestrials' own fault if they
get hurt, Adam thought. They started it.

Now in sight of Pilgrim Park the boys got quiet.

"We'll just go and get settled in the clubhouse,"
Adam said softly. "When we get inside, I want all
you guys to lie down on your stomachs and face the
doorway. Get ready. As soon as we hear those guys
coming, you know what to do."

"Noise," said Hector. "We make all the noise we
can."

"Right," said Adam. "If we want to win, we have
to surprise them and get them fast."

"Fast," everyone agreed.

"We're going to win," said Adam. "I know it."

"Sure," all the Angels said. "We're going to win."

Adam led the way inside the wrought iron gate, past the faded sign that said PILGRIM PARK.

From a distance he heard a church bell strike the hour—nine tones rang out. Nine o'clock on Saturday morning, Adam thought, as if later he would tell about this day, like in the classroom when people had to get up and give a talk, "My Summer Vacation" or "My Most Exciting Moment."

This was sure to be an exciting day, Adam thought. Excitement made everything quiver. The autumn leaves leapt on the branches. The little kids swung higher and faster on the swings than ever before. Now, moving toward his bench, the veteran was stepping briskly, his husky beside him like a guard dog on duty.

The man and the dog sat down in their usual place, and Adam thought he saw the veteran gaze at him and nod his head up and down. For a moment Adam hesitated. It seemed almost like the veteran wanted to speak to him. As Adam walked past the bench, he heard the man muttering. He couldn't make out the words. The beautiful dog sat up tall, its ears erect. Adam hurried on. His friends were following.

He turned up the path toward the big maple tree, where the clubhouse stood with its sign, ANGELS, and the word beneath it, STINKS.

Hector ran up beside Adam. His eyes glowed with

excitement. "We're gonna cream them!" Hector whispered happily.

They neared the clubhouse. The thing sagged. The plywood was stained and scratched. The cloth hung limply at the doorway; the roof, made of a piece of tin, seemed about to cave in.

It didn't look like such a great clubhouse, Adam thought. It was really too small. They could build a much better clubhouse at the other side of the park if they all worked together. They could get stuff from the junk piles and trash dumpsters. It would be fun.

As Adam glanced back at his friends, he saw the excitement in their faces, their bodies ready for action. It was impossible now to turn back. Adam lifted his arm for a signal. Brendan, bringing up the rear, gave Adam an OK sign.

Everyone gathered close around Adam.

"Act normal," Adam whispered, "in case there are any spies around. Do you see anybody?"

"No," they all shook their heads.

"So, we'll go on in," Adam said. "Once we get inside, we keep absolutely quiet, and we wait. Got it?"

"Got it," they all said, and they began to move very quietly, following their leader.

Adam took a deep breath. He stepped out toward the clubhouse. Adam pushed aside the cloth curtain.

Screams suddenly filled the air, loud and desperate

and shrill. Everything was a blur, the sounds, the feelings, the fear. The Terrestrials came rushing out of the clubhouse. They screamed and yelled. They swung their sticks and aimed their rocks, they hurled themselves at the Angels. And with them was Jamie Rand.

"Fink!" Adam screamed. "Spy!"

Now he was really ready for war.

NINE

The War

Adam shouted orders. "Take cover! Over there! Come on! Come on!"

The Terrestrials tried to surround them, waving sticks, hurling stones, yelling threats.

The Angels ran back, hiding behind bushes, ducking in and out of benches, racing behind the trash bin.

Adam, crouched behind a shrub, felt his heart pounding. He glanced up and saw Hector lighting a firecracker, panting so hard his hands were shaking.

He saw Mike behind the tree, aiming his coffee can filled with stones, and Brendan beside him, trying to arm his slingshot.

Arlo, the big muscle man, lay on his belly, taking cover. Jamie Rand was jumping up and down, screaming. Wes and Troy kept racing around the clubhouse, grabbing onto stuff, until the hut shook and sagged and seemed about to collapse.

Adam thought, they're just as scared of us as we are of them.

Things seemed to slow down. It seemed almost as if music were playing somewhere in the background, a slow, gliding tune. Rocks flew, but they also seemed to float; someone screamed, and slowly a fist was raised, a stick was hurled, a foot kicked out. Troy's face was suddenly close to Adam's. In a moment it vanished. Someone lay on top of Adam; the weight was huge, as if a building had come down on top of him. Then Adam was on his feet again, and he was swinging, kicking, punching, shouting.

People were screaming from far away. A woman called out, "Stop them! Stop them!"

It seemed to shake Adam back to the present. His ribs hurt but he was OK.

Then Adam realized that there were only five Terrestrials. There was Troy. There was Wes. There were Arlo and Jerry and Jamie. Carl was missing.

What great luck!

Adam shouted out their battle cry. "Angels! Assault!"

And then, right behind his head Adam heard a click.

Adam turned slowly. There was a sudden stillness. Time seemed to hang like heat in the air.

First Adam saw only the dark metal, a long tube. Then he saw the wood. Then the word came to him. *Rifle.*

Everything seemed astonishingly clear.

Adam heard the little kids laughing and yelling from the swings.

He smelled the leaves from the maple tree.

He saw the sharp crease in the veteran's cap, and he saw the way the husky sat and panted, his ears erect, sides quivering with each breath.

Carl stood just behind Adam, with the rifle aimed. The click of the rifle seemed to echo in Adam's ears.

Far behind Carl stood Jerry, his face frozen into a weird grin.

Strange words came from nowhere—*hurry! hurry!*

Adam leapt and threw himself at Carl.

Next, he tasted salt and felt a coldness upon him, heard the crash of thunder, and he fell back with Carl on top of him.

It seemed like a long time, but it was only a moment. The air had been split apart by the sound of a shot. Everything stopped.

And then things started moving again. Adam

picked himself up. Behind him he became aware of the other boys, Angels and Terrestrials, getting up, gathering themselves together. He became aware of moans, howls, terrible sounds coming from the bench where the veteran sat with his dog.

Adam ran toward the bench. The veteran was doubled over now, one knee on the ground.

On the ground Adam saw a pool of blood. It spread further and further into the dirt. The beautiful husky lay on his side, legs still jerking, mouth wide open and oozing.

Adam saw, through his sudden tears, the face of the veteran, closer than he had ever seen it before, saw lines and shadows, saw darkness and grief so deep and so real that he knew he would never forget it, just as he would never forget the sound of the trigger, the click.

Adam stood there trembling. He felt cold and hot both at the same time, unable to move.

At last Adam turned and saw that nearly everyone had gone. Angels and Terrestrials, as one, had run away. Only Hector stood there, twisting his hands over and over, his mouth wide open, and he was crying.

Adam's lips felt puffed and sore. He reached toward the veteran, and he spoke. It came out in a whisper.

"I'm sorry," Adam said.

The veteran's head bobbed up and down, up and down, as he bent over the dog. Tears covered his face and ran into his mouth. "Dead, oh, dead. Dead, oh, dead. He's dead. War. Kills."

Later there were sirens and a white truck. All the grown-ups in the park had gathered. A policeman came. Somehow Adam got home. People talked and pointed and explained. Adam's dad nodded and nodded, as if he knew all about it.

But nobody could know Adam's pain.

TEN

Some Other Day

Conversations crisscrossed the rooms; Adam heard every word. They all had things to say, his mother, his dad, his aunt, the neighbors.

"Well, boys will be boys."

"It started out innocently."

"It was just a game."

"I didn't think kids played war anymore."

"Are you kidding?"

"Well, who could know that such a thing would happen?"

"It's a miracle one of the children wasn't shot."

"They say that rifle was pointed toward the swings."

"A good thing Adam jumped on that boy."

"People shouldn't keep guns. You see what happens."

"Listen, with crime like it is, decent people need to protect themselves."

"I'd never keep a loaded gun, that's for sure."

"What will happen to that boy?"

"He'll have to be punished."

"That poor old guy. That dog was all he had."

"Who is he?"

"Just some old soldier, sits in the park all day. Name's Brown, according to the police. Sylvester Brown."

"What's a guy like that do all day long?"

"Who knows? The boys say he just hangs around— sort of creepy."

"They should keep bums out of the park."

"The guy meant no harm."

"Parks aren't safe anymore. Somebody should do something. This is terrible."

Adam woke up very early on Sunday morning. He had fallen asleep before dinner the night before, and he couldn't even remember getting into bed or dreaming. He felt like a stone, a thing without feelings, numb.

His mom was already in the kitchen, stirring her coffee round and round. She looked up when Adam entered, and softly she said, "Hi."

"I have to go and talk to the old man," Adam said.

"What old man?"

"The veteran. I have to tell him."

"What in the world can you tell him?"

Adam shrugged. His dad came in, poured himself coffee, and with a sigh, sat down.

"Do you want me to go with you, Son?"

"No," Adam said.

"But it's not as if you shot the dog," said Adam's mom.

"It was my club," Adam said. "I started the war."

"You're not responsible when other kids get crazy," said his dad.

Adam shrugged. "I want to go see him," he repeated.

Adam's mom frowned. "Do you know where he lives?"

"Colton Street," Adam replied.

"Oh, Adam, I don't think . . ." his mom began.

"Let him go, Sylvia," said Adam's dad.

"But you don't know anything about this man!" she objected.

"Adam knows enough," said his dad.

They talked on and on. And Adam felt filled with the sound of their voices, their arguments. He left quietly by the back door.

The streets were misty with Sunday silence; it was cold. A few early churchgoers passed by, walking swiftly. Otherwise, Adam felt the chill of being entirely alone.

He walked one block, then another, and found himself in front of Hector's house. Within, it was strangely quiet. Adam knocked. Hector came to the door. When he saw Adam, he broke into a grin, swiftly gone.

"Who's that, Hector?" came his father's voice, stern and strong.

"Uh—nobody. Just the—the paper." Hector bent down and scooped up the Sunday paper, tucked it under his arm. "My dad's real mad about what happened," Hector said. "He won't let me go anywhere. He won't let me do anything. He says we're all too rowdy."

Adam nodded. "I was going to see the old veteran," he said. "On Colton Street," he added. "I thought you'd want to come with me. We could—well." Adam sighed. "We could say we're sorry. You know. Maybe help him with something. He must feel awful."

Hector frowned doubtfully. Then he said, "I'll ask," and he ducked back inside.

It seemed a long, long time that Hector was gone. At last he emerged, wearing his jacket and a cap. "OK," he said.

"You can come?" Adam exclaimed. For the first time since yesterday morning he felt a little better.

"My folks said it's the right thing to do. But they said we better be back right away, or else. I have to be home in an hour. Or else."

The boys walked in near silence the seven blocks to Colton Street. There seemed nothing more to say; the events of yesterday needed no words, no reasons or explanations. What had happened had simply happened, that was all.

As Adam walked along, he felt cold. The wind whipped bundles of leaves up around his ankles. He tucked his hands deep into his pockets. He led the way, five blocks to the right, then left two blocks to Colton Street. The old soldier's home was the second building from the corner, tucked between a dreary dark delicatessen, with rooms above it, and a dry goods store, now covered with a metal gate and padlocked.

Several men prowled on the corner, talking together and smoking. A boy whizzed past on a skateboard.

Adam pulled Hector into the dark doorway. He scanned the names on the register, peering closely, going from top to bottom twice before he saw the name scrawled in heavy ink: SYLV. BROWN.

"There it is," Hector whispered. He pressed the bell.

They waited. No buzzer, no voice, nothing.

Adam pressed the bell and again the boys waited.

The glass door swung open. There stood the veteran, dressed in a long, dark bathrobe, without his cap, and a gray towel flung around his neck.

Hector gasped and grabbed Adam's arm.

The veteran stared at the boys, gazing from one to the other, as if they were strange animals, suddenly appeared from nowhere.

"Hi," said Adam.

The man made a sound, less than a word.

"We came to talk to you," said Adam.

"Yeah," said Hector.

"OK," said the veteran. He peered at the boys intently, his neck stretched forward, eyes bright.

"I—I—I'm so sorry!" Adam burst out. "I thought—I want to tell you I liked your dog so much. He was so beautiful. And smart. I could see how smart he was. And now—I thought we could— maybe you are going to have a funeral. Maybe we could help you. Maybe you'll get another dog."

"We could go with you to the pound," Hector put in, his voice trembling.

"Yes! Yes!" exclaimed Adam. "Maybe we could help you pay for the puppy's shots. We—we want to help."

"No," said the man.

"No?"

"It's all been done."

"You—buried General?" Adam suddenly felt lost.

"It's all been done," the man repeated.

"What about another dog?" Adam persisted. "A puppy. You could get a puppy."

"No," said the veteran.

Adam gazed across the street, where a man was picking through a trash can. Hector stood there, silent and sagging. Adam had never seen his friend looking so miserable.

For a long moment Adam could think of nothing else to say or do.

Suddenly the man spoke. "Want to come in?" he asked. "Into my place? I have a picture. Of General."

Adam felt a lump in his throat, fear more than sorrow. Go inside? Be trapped, maybe? Adam looked at Hector; his eyes were wide. He was waiting for Adam to decide.

"Sure," Adam said. "We can only stay a minute."

The veteran turned and led the way down a dark hall, then up one flight of stairs. He took a large key out of the pocket of his robe and carefully unlocked the door, opened it, and went inside.

The boys followed.

It was a large room with a kitchen counter and a stove at the far end, everything tidy and clean but worn. The rug was worn flat, and the sofa had been carefully patched with various squares of cloth. And Adam wondered whether General, as a pup, had perhaps chewed the sofa, and then he decided no, no way.

Now the veteran turned and went to a low wooden cabinet that stood against a wall. On top was a photograph of the husky, sitting proudly on the sidewalk out front.

"Oh," said Hector, a whisper, almost like a cry.

"He was beautiful," said Adam.

The veteran picked up the photograph and handed it to Adam

"Here," he said. "Take it."

"What?" Adam drew back. "No, no, it's yours. I shouldn't take it. I mean, you'll want it to remember him by."

The veteran shook his head, over and over. "No. I don't need it. You take it." He pressed the photograph into Adam's hands, tight against Adam's chest. "It's yours."

The photograph felt like a living thing in Adam's hands, like something that might breathe and move. The dog looked so real.

"I—I—I," Adam stammered. "Thank—thank you, Mr. Brown."

"We better go," said Hector.

Suddenly Adam felt a hand on his shoulder, warm

and heavy. The man stood close beside Adam, and it seemed that Adam could feel the very breath moving through his body.

"What's your name?" asked the veteran, staring at Adam.

"Adam. And this is Hector."

"Some other day," said the veteran, his voice clear now, like a bell.

Adam glanced up into the man's eyes. They were deep and watery, like a deep well. "Some other day?"

"Maybe at the park." The veteran nodded. "We'll see."

Adam glanced at Hector. Unspoken questions bounced between them. What did the man mean, "some other day"? What *could* he mean, except that they might meet again, perhaps on better terms, in a happier time.

"We better go," Hector said again. His voice was low and hoarse.

The veteran nodded and walked with them down the stairs, through the dark hallway, and to the front door.

Down on the sidewalk Adam and Hector took a few steps, then stopped. They turned to look back. The veteran was gone.

"The guys will never believe this," said Hector. "He gave us a *picture*. Of his *dog*. I guess he doesn't hate us."

"I guess not," said Adam.

Above, some clouds had crowded together in the sky. They looked like snow clouds.

Adam could still feel the touch of the man's hand upon him.

With a sudden burst of energy Adam turned to his friend.

"Let's race back to your house!" he yelled.

"Ready! Go!"

Adam ran and ran and ran, as if he were flying, as if he could fly straight up into that bright new day. As he ran, Adam clutched the photograph tight to his chest. It was something he would keep forever.